The Bramblefrost Fairies

BY

C. A. FOWER

Published by New Generation Publishing in 2013

Copyright © Clare Fower 2013

First Edition

The author asserts the moral right under the Copyright, Designs and Patents Act 1988 to be identified as the author of this work.

All Rights reserved. No part of this publication may be reproduced, stored in a retrieval system or transmitted, in any form or by any means without the prior consent of the author, nor be otherwise circulated in any form of binding or cover other than that which it is published and without a similar condition being imposed on the subsequent purchaser.

www.newgeneration-publishing.com

 **New Generation Publishing**

ACKNOWLEDGEMENTS

I would like to dedicate this book to the following:

My beloved Mum and Dad who I miss every day.

Gone but never forgotten.

My wonderful husband Dave, without whom this book would not have been published.

And to my treasured family, my dear son Adam, and my much loved nieces and nephews, for whom this book was written, you're my inspiration.

And finally my close friends, you know who you are.

THANK YOU

Chapter One

SPRING AND NEW BEGINNINGS

"As I work inside your house, quiet and silent as a mouse, I bid you all to soundly sleep and through your eyes you must not peep, until my job I've been and done, then you may waken with the sun."

There was a soft crackle, which echoed around the house, as the sleep enchantment took effect.

"If we don't hurry, the sun will definitely be up before we've done," said Twotone.

"Yes but that's three teeth in one night, not bad going," replied Muddy as he slipped a rather big tooth into the tooth pouch, "Granit will be pleased."

"Come on boys, we need to go, the sun is going to rise soon, and we've got to be out of the village before it does," came a voice from behind them as Shade and Shimmer crept into the room.

As the sun rose, the four fairies were well on their way home. They are tooth fairies and use children's teeth as bricks to build their houses. They live in a little village of their own, right in the heart of the English countryside, beneath a particularly thick hedgerow, which marks the boundary of Bramblefrost Manor, a fine Georgian manor house that has changed little with the passing of time. They are very lucky to live where they do, and are the envy of many villages, as the Manor provides very well for all their needs, with its walled garden set for vegetables no matter what the season and the orchards full of fruit trees and bushes. The Manor itself is quite a long way up a windy gravel drive, and so the fairies are left in peace to do their own thing.

"I think spring is on the way," remarked Shimmer as the four entered the village and began to walk along the dotted paths between each little house.

"Yes" agreed Shade. "The nights are shorter; we only just made it back before dawn tonight,"

"Very true, I know your sleep enchantments are strong, Shade, but even they will break with the dawn, we must be more careful," said Twotone, a little concerned.

"We're back ok though," announced Muddy, sounding not in the least bit concerned about getting caught, "and Granit can't be cross, when he sees we've brought back three teeth, and good ones too."

"Even the bounty of collecting three teeth, is not worth getting caught for, Muddy!" came a soft but firm voice. Granit, who was the elder of Bramblefrost village, and was very wise, came from behind one of the little houses carrying a lantern.

Muddy looked a bit embarrassed, and said, "No, I suppose it isn't, we will be more careful from now on."

"Good" replied Granit, "Though I must say, you four have done very well. Three teeth you say, surely not from one village?"

"No," said Shimmer, "We visited three." She turned to Shade and said, "Shade's sleep enchantments are getting better, really strong."

"Yes." Granit's eyes fell upon Shade. "I have

noticed, you seem to have a gift for enchantments my dear," he said, and then he turned and looked at the others. "Well, I will keep you no longer, but remember next time you four go out, you must be more aware." And with that he headed off towards the entrance of the village.

"Where do you think Granit is going so early?" remarked Muddy as they strolled towards Shade and Shimmer's little house.

"I bet he's going over to the Meadowsweet village it's that time of year again, all the elders from the local villages meet, to discuss the coming year, don't they?"

The Meadowsweet village was the nearest neighbour to the Bramblefrost village. They were not tooth fairies, they were Moorland fairies, and lived in an old rabbit warren, hidden by trees on the hills beyond the fields of the Bramblefrost Manor estate, which was only about five minutes away as the crow or fairy flies.

"Oh yes of course, the big meeting for the year ahead, and the coming celebrations no doubt," replied Muddy with a big smile on his face.

The girls laughed and Shimmer said, "Trust you to think of that, Muddy."

"What's wrong with that, any excuse for a party I say, what do you say Twotone?"

Twotone just shook his head and smiled, "Come on, let's leave the girls to it, it's been a hard day's night," and with that the boys headed off through the big hedge and home.

Candlemas

It was early February and Granit announced that a very important fairy celebration called Candlemas was to take place at the Meadowsweet village hall. Twotone was given the task of making the candles, and was busy heating wax and pouring it into little sand moulds.

"I've brought you some carrot soup," said Muddy as he came into the workshop. "Have you got many more to make?"

"Not many now," replied Twotone, "It's a good job really, going to need more wax soon!"

"Oh right," said Muddy, "Need bees for that then, don't mind if we get that job, good perks, honey!"

Twotone smiled and said, "Yes I suppose so, should be a good party, by all accounts the Meadowsweet lot throw a good bash."

"Can't wait," replied Muddy, "Shade and Shimmer are making some of the cakes for the celebration, and they said they would make us a small batch too, you know, just to make sure they are nice tasting."

Twotone smiled and ate his carrot soup.

When Muddy and Twotone arrived, Meadowsweet hall was getting full, but they saw Shade and Shimmer among the crowd, making their way to the table on which stood all the cakes.

"Hope these cakes are ok," said Shimmer as she placed her two trays on the table with all the others.

"They'll be fine," replied Shade, "No one makes a better fairy cake than you. Shimmer."

"Very true, we can vouch for that," came a voice from behind them.

"Well thank you Muddy," said Shimmer with a smile. "Did you manage to make all the candles, Twotone?"

"Yes, just about had enough wax. I've told Granit we will have to get some more."

"Good job spring is on the way then, at least the bees will be busy before too long now," replied Shimmer.

Just then Granit and Heather, who was the elder of the Meadowsweet village, came into the room and asked for silence.

"May I have your attention for a moment," said Heather in a calm voice, "I would like to first of all welcome our good friends and neighbours from the Bramblefrost village. Thank you all for celebrating Candlemas with us, and for your kind donations of food, wine and of course the allimportant cakes and candles. This is one of my favourite celebrations, as it marks the start of spring, and new beginnings. Now as tradition has it, we must ice the cakes with white icing, which has been done, and place white candles upon them, which my good friend Granit is doing right now. On each candle he places a blessing for the coming year, when all the candles are lit."

She looked towards Granit, who smiled and nodded.

"We can all line up and Granit will hand you each a cake, then I hope you will all join me in blowing out your candles and making your own wishes for the year ahead. Thank you."

There was a huge cheer and everyone clapped and formed a line around the room, and when everyone had been handed their cake, they formed a big circle around Granit and Heather, and silence fell around the room once more.

Granit then stepped forward and said:

"As the first signs of spring begin to appear, both in the meadows and the hedgerows, we send out our blessings for the coming year. May you all go forth in love and light."

With that everyone blew out their candles as wishes were made, and another loud cheer filled the hall.

"Thank you Granit," said Heather with a bow and a big smile, then turning to everyone she said, "I hope all your wishes come true," and the music began to play.

"Care for a dance anyone?" asked Muddy as he stuffed the last piece of his cake into his mouth.

"Let us eat our cake first Muddy," laughed

Shimmer.

"Yeah," remarks Twotone, "we don't all eat as fast as you. It's a wonder you don't get indigestion!"

Muddy just smiled and said, "Indigestion, what's that?"

The others shook their heads, and then Shade bowed low and said,

"May I have the pleasure of the next dance, Twotone?"

He smiled a shy smile, then took Shade's hand and said in a low voice,

"The pleasure is mine."

"Just leaves us then," said Muddy with a cheeky grin on his face.

"So it seems," giggled Shimmer, as she took his hand.

The party went on until the early hours, and as Shade, Shimmer, Muddy and Twotone made their way home, the moon was full and shone brightly, lighting up the whole countryside before them.

"That was a great celebration", remarked Shade, "I hope that's the start of a good year."

"Is that what you wished for then, Shade?" asked Muddy

"I can't tell you what I wished for, or it won't come true, as well you know Muddy Mischief!" replied Shade.

"Ok, don't get your wings in a flap, just wondered that's all," said Muddy with a grin, "Muddy Mischief eh, now I AM wondering what you wished for."

Shade seemed a little embarrassed and changed the subject.

"Nice little village isn't it, Meadowsweet, curious little passages everywhere."

"Yes," replied Twotone, "wish we had a village hall like theirs, it would be useful in winter, might suggest it to Granit."

"Oh right," said Muddy "So we all know what you wished for then, Twotone."

Twotone just smiled and said, "Now that would be telling, wouldn't it Muddy?"

"Well I don't care what you all wished for," announced Shimmer, "I agree with Shade. It was a good celebration, and spring is on the way, as Heather so rightly put it, a new beginning, so let's hope that it is the start of a good year ahead for us all."

CHAPTER TWO

IN BROAD DAYLIGHT

It was summer at Bramblefrost Manor, which was generally a lazy time of year for the fairies, as the only things they had to do were to collect the teeth from the children in local villages and put them into storage, and so you could say that this was the holiday season.

This summer was promising to be a good one. The sun was blazing and everyone felt quite happy and contented to just sit around in the fields beyond the hedge, and have their picnics and the odd game of cricket, and in the warm evenings they would all gather on the other side of the hedge, in the grounds of Bramblefrost Manor, where across a small well-kept lawn, there stood a magnificent weeping willow. The whole village would meet there every night, to sing and dance beneath its flowing branches.

Twotone, Muddy, Shade and Shimmer always loved the gatherings, for it was at one of these that Muddy suggested they should all meet the following day, and go exploring up at the Manor.

"What, in broad daylight?" exclaimed Shimmer. "What if someone should see us?"

"They won't, we'll be careful, Oh come on, it'll be fun."

Looking at each other doubtfully, the others agreed.

The next morning, quite early it was, before the sun got too high, and the rest of the village was even awake, the four fairies crept very quietly out of the village, and headed off towards the back of Bramblefrost Manor.

"Somehow this feels a bit naughty," said Twotone as they crept along the windy little paths between the flower borders,

"I know what you mean," replied Shade.

"As Shimmer said, we really shouldn't be out in broad daylight!"

"Oh rubbish," said Muddy, "where's your sense of adventure? Anyhow I bet the family isn't even there, I bet they are on holiday."

"Well, even if they are," said Twotone, "that doesn't mean the house will be deserted, they have got a house full of servants you know."

"Yes," said Shimmer, "not to mention the gardener, we'd better keep our eyes open for him!"

"Don't worry," replied Muddy, "they won't even be

up yet."

And so the four fairies, feeling a bit more secure in the knowledge that the household would still be asleep, crept ever closer to the tall grass at the edge of the big lawn.

"How about we make our way to the pond on the other side of the big lawn?" suggested Muddy. "Perhaps the fountain will be on, and we can have our lunch there."

"What a good idea," agreed the others. "There doesn't seem to be anyone around, so we could have a swim to cool off."

By now, the sun was getting very warm.

As the four fairies approached the pond they were excited to see the fountain was on, and being rather hot, they decided to go and have a look to see if it was safe for a swim. Muddy and Twotone suggested the girls wait for them in the camouflage of the shrubs surrounding the pond, while they checked it out.

"OK, coast is clear!" shouted Twotone to the girls, and so they all stood at the edge of the pond in anticipation.

"You first," said Twotone to Muddy, and with that Muddy flew gracefully up into the air, and dive bombed straight into the water. "Wow that's great" he laughed as he bubbled to the surface, "Come on in."

None of them had to be asked twice, they all jumped in and proceeded to splash around in and out of the fountain, and down to the bottom of the pond, coming up and resting on the broad lily pads, which dipped gracefully on top of the water. Muddy and Twotone found it great fun to slide down the neck of the fountain and plop into the water. It was so hot now, that they were only too grateful to cool off.

As the morning wore on they seemed to be oblivious to the comings and goings of the gardener. Unfortunately he was not oblivious to the splashes coming from the pond, and so decided to investigate.

As the gardener grew closer to the pond, he stopped, for he could not believe his eyes. "Perhaps," he thought to himself, "I have spent too much time in the sun." And he began to rub his eyes, but sure enough, when he looked again, he could still see them.

"Well I'll be jiggered!" he announced out loud, without realising it.

The four fairies looked around in alarm, and

suddenly realised, that they were in great danger, as their wings were wet and they could not fly.

"RUN," shouted Muddy and Twotone together, but as the boys sprang from the top of the fountain and into the bushes, the gardener was placing a plant pot over the two girls and exclaiming, "You two can come with me, or no one will believe a word I say!" And with that he strode off towards the house.

The Capture

"What are we going to do?" exclaimed Muddy pulling bits of leaves and twigs from his hair, "It's all my fault, I wanted to come here, and now Shade and Shimmer are captured, and who knows what will happen to them?"

"We must not panic!" replied Twotone,

sounding extremely panicked, and beating his wings so frantically in order to dry them, that he didn't notice that he had taken off. It was a stroke of luck that he did, because he saw the gardener go into the manor by the back entrance, before he came crashing down.

"Flipping heck, are you OK?" said Muddy, as Twotone lay in a big heap on the floor.

"Yes, yes" said Twotone, leaping to his feet, "Come on, I know where he has taken them."

Meanwhile the girls kept very still and quiet in their plant pot prison, and listened to the gardener telling the head maid what he had just witnessed. "Don't be silly, George" she said in a kind voice, "There's no such thing as fairies, you haven't been in the cocktail cabinet or cook's cooking sherry have you?"

"No," replied George, "I must admit, I too thought I had spent too long in the sun, but just you look in here."

With that the gardener carefully placed the plant pot into a big mixing bowl, and lightly tapped the upturned bottom. The two fairies dropped out into the bowl, and the gardener quickly placed a muslin cloth over the top. "There what did I tell you, don't think I am off my rocker now, do you?"

The maid stood motionless with her mouth wide open.

"Oh my, George!" she exclaimed. "What are you going to do with them, they look so frightened."

"I know they do," said George, quite concerned. "I don't want to frighten the poor little things."

You see, luckily for Shade and Shimmer, old

George the gardener would not hurt a fly, but he had to show somebody what he had seen, so that he knew he hadn't lost his marbles.

"I thought I heard fairies once or twice in the evenings, when I was closing up the wood shed and so on, but I never thought I'd see one."

"Well what to do," said the maid, looking at Shade and Shimmer with a kind face. "I know, how about we borrow Miss Hayley's dolls house, she won't be any the wiser, being on holiday and all, anyway I don't think she would really mind, if she knew why we had used it."

"What," replied George, "You are not thinking of keeping them are you?"

"No," said the maid, "I just think they would be more comfortable in there until we think what we are going to do with them,"

"Well, I'll tell you what we are not going to do, and that is show them to anyone else. They belong outside, as free as the birds, not as someone's pets!"

"George, you should know me better than that," said the maid in rather a stern voice, "of course we will release them, but not now. I really don't know what they are doing out in broad daylight. I say we give them something to eat and settle them down in the doll's house until this evening, then we can take them down to the back of the Aviary, and away from any prying eyes, and set them free."

"Good idea", said old George, very relieved.

Shade and Shimmer listened to the conversation with great relief, but didn't say a word.

The Doll's House

The maid picked up the heavy mixing bowl, and

announced, "Come along sweethearts, let's get you upstairs out of harm's way."

She proceeded out of the servants' kitchen through a rather large door, and up a narrow winding staircase. When they reached the top they turned left, down equally narrow corridors, passing several doorways, until, "Here we are," and she opened the door into a huge, bright, colourful bedroom.

"This is Miss Hayley's room," said the maid cheerfully.

As the fairies looked around them, they saw what a beautiful room it was. The walls were covered in bright yellow, with a deep colourful border of none other than fairies, dancing around the big room. It had a huge white fireplace on one wall and on the facing wall was a wonderful carved pine bedstead, with the most beautiful lace bedspread upon it. The room had a huge bay window, from which hung equally beautiful heavy lace curtains, tied up to hooks on each side, which made them drop down elegantly onto a brightly polished wooden floor. And set on a lace-covered table in one corner of the room stood the most magnificent doll's house.

The maid set down the bowl carefully on Miss Hayley's dressing table, and went to open up the front of the doll's house, then she took the bowl and tipped it slightly, so that the fairies could quite easily slide out of it, and into the lounge of the doll's house.

"There we are, safe and sound," said the maid in a calming voice. "I bet you are hungry aren't you, now let me see, what do fairies eat? I know!"

she exclaimed excitedly. "I bet you would like a nice cheese sandwich and a small slice of cook's sugar topped fruit cake," and with that she scurried off back through the door.

"Well," said Shade quite matter of factly, "What an adventure this has turned out to be. I bet the boys are beside themselves with worry."

"I bet," said Shimmer, "That will teach us to go out in broad daylight without our wits about us. It's a good thing that it was old George the gardener who spotted us, otherwise who knows where we would have ended up."

"Still," said Shade, "no need to panic, we know they mean us no harm, so let's just relax, and enjoy ourselves. I don't think any of the village has ever visited Miss Hayley's room, have they?"

"I don't believe so," replied Shimmer, "no one

has ever mentioned it at story time or at the gatherings, which means I suppose, that either she doesn't believe in fairies, which I find unlikely, being as how her bedroom is covered in them, or she has very strong teeth, in which case, we will be very pleased to visit this room again."

"Yes," said Shade giggling, "but next time at night when everyone's asleep."

Just then the door opened, and in walked the maid carrying a small tray on which was placed a cheese sandwich, which she had cut into little squares without the crusts and, as she put it, "a small slice of sugary fruit cake," and a small glass of homemade lemonade. She then took two serving dishes, two exquisite wine glasses, and one jug from the kitchen of the doll's house and then divided the cake in half, and tipped the lemonade into the jug.

"Here we are," she said as she placed everything on the dining room table. "Eat up and I'll see you later, you'll be quite safe here, so don't be afraid."

And with that she made her way back out of the room.

Shade and Shimmer sat down at the big table in the dining room of the doll's house, and began to tuck into the sandwich, closely followed by the fruitcake.

"Oh, I don't think I have ever tasted anything as nice as this!" said Shimmer, trying not to drop one single crumb of the fruitcake.

"My word, no," laughed Shade. "It's definitely worth being captured for, and this lemonade is something else too."

When the girls had eaten and drunk all they could, they decided to explore the doll's house. First of all they went from the dining room into a well-furnished kitchen. It had everything your heart could desire— solid wooden cupboards with brass handles containing everything from pots and pans to cutlery, and in one corner of the kitchen stood a beautiful glass fronted dresser, containing a bone china dinner service decorated with elegant pink rosebuds.

"Oh wow," exclaimed Shimmer, "How wonderful."

Next they went through an oak panelled door into the hall, which was decorated with little floral tiles and led to the carved oak staircase. There were two other doors from the hall into a study and the main lounge, which was furnished with a large sumptuous suite with plump cushions scattered upon it. A huge tiled fire place stood on the main wall, complete with a brass coal scuttle full of tiny pieces of coal on one side of the hearth, and a basket of logs on the other. The facing wall contained a huge bay window made from real leaded glass with tiny hooks to open it, and hung from it were richly coloured heavy velvet curtains. The two girls were impressed.

"Thought of everything, haven't they?" said Shade.

"I could live here myself."

"Yes." agreed Shimmer, "So could I."

The girls then decided to have a wander up the stairs, where they found four doors, the first one leading into a large bathroom containing a wonderful shaped enamel bath. The other three were bedrooms— a double, a single, and a nursery. All three were bright and cheerful, with wardrobes and chests of drawers containing very well-tailored clothes. The girls' faces lit up, and as they browsed through some of the exquisite dresses, they lost track of time and before they knew it the light was fading.

"When do you think the maid will come and set us free?" asked Shimmer, a little concerned.

"Oh I am sure she won't be long," said Shade, "after all, she and old George did say they would wait until dark because of prying eyes, didn't they?"

"Yes," replied Shimmer, feeling a little guilty for enjoying herself, "But what about the boys, I bet they are going nuts with worry!"

She was right of course. The boys had spent the

afternoon searching for the girls and getting themselves all worked up because they couldn't find them. Of course they didn't know that old George and the maid were going to set the girls free— for all they knew, they could be keeping them, or even worse, showing them to the whole world.

By now the light was fading and the village would soon be gathering beneath the willow tree, and they would surely be missed.

"Where could they be?" asked Muddy with a nervous voice.

"I don't know!" replied Twotone, "but I say we just keep our eyes on that gardener, he is sure to have hidden them somewhere. I think we should stay here and watch that door until he appears."

"Oh all right," said Muddy, "but if we don't find

them soon, we are in big trouble!"

Just about then, as if she'd heard everything that had been said, the maid came scurrying through the big door into Miss Hayley's room.

"Are you OK in there?" she asked, as she peered in through the windows. "Come along, it's time to go."

With that she slowly opened the side of the house up and reached in. She then carefully took the two fairies in her hand, and popped them both back into the mixing bowl, placing the cloth back over the top, then she tidied up the doll's house and put everything back in its place.

"There now, no one will ever know," she announced as she picked up the mixing bowl and made her way back out of the room, and down the corridors and winding staircase, into the kitchen where old George stood waiting for them.

"Come on then, are they all right?" asked George, peering into the bowl.

"Of course they are!" replied the maid, "They have eaten all that cake, and drank all the lemonade, so I don't think they must have been too frightened, in fact I might go as far as to say they enjoyed their little stay in the doll's house. It's been like a holiday for them I expect."

"Yes," said George, "I suppose it has. Well let's get them back outside, where they belong, eh?"

And with that, old George and the maid took the mixing bowl and proceeded out of the kitchen and into the garden.

"Look, there they are!" exclaimed Muddy excitedly.

"Yes," said Twotone, "come on, we have to

follow and see where they are taking them."

The two boys were astonished to see the gardener and the maid take the girls to the bottom of the garden behind the Aviary.

"Well," said George, "I don't suppose anyone will ever believe us, will they, but who cares, we know we are not bonkers." And with that he lifted the cloth from the bowl and said, "Off you go then, and be more careful next time you venture out in broad daylight."

"Just a minute," said the maid, "I have something for you to remember us by," and she produced the two tiny cut glass wine glasses they had used in the doll's house. The two fairies flew gracefully up and landed on the hand of the kind faced maid, and said "Thank you."

Then turning to old George they said, "We will

never be afraid of you again, and we will never forget your kindness."

With that they flew up into the air, and disappeared over the hedge, closely followed by Twotone and Muddy.

"Look," said George, "more of them," and he and the maid smiled at each other as they walked back to the house, but they didn't say another word.

CHAPTER THREE

AUTUMN AT BRAMBLEFROST

As into autumn we go, and the days grow ever shorter, Granit begins to make plans for the coming winter.

"It is going to be a severe winter this year," he warned on this particular occasion . "The trees are already preparing for it, and so must we."

This meant that the fairies of Bramblefrost would have to go deep into the forest to collect dry wood which they needed to make into charcoal. The fairies use this as their main source of heating, as it has no smoke, which might be seen for miles and give away the location of the village.

Muddy Twotone, Shade and Shimmer formed a

group as usual, and Granit instructed them to collect their wood at the far end of the forest, near the waterfall. The four fairies know that they would need help bringing the wood back to the village, so they set off for a nearby field to enlist the help of two rabbits who lived there, called Pepper and Romany.

It took quite some time to reach the waterfall, so the fairies began to gather the dry wood, while the rabbits rested.

"Don't you think that we are doing this too early?" asked Muddy.

"Well, Granit must know what he is doing," replied Shade.

"Better to be safe than sorry, I suppose," said Twotone, rather seriously. "After all, we wouldn't want to run out of charcoal in the middle of a bitter winter, would we?"

"No," agreed the others, the very thought of it making them shiver.

The four fairies worked very hard all day, until evening fell. By then they had gathered a big pile of wood, which they wrapped up into two big bundles.

"Do you think it's wise to set off back to the village tonight?" asked Shimmer, a little concerned. "I am only thinking of the rabbits, you know, foxes and suchlike."

"Yes of course," said Twotone, "how stupid of us, we'd better look for a suitable shelter for the night!"

The rabbits, I must say, were starting to get a little worried, as the mist was creeping along the forest floor, making it hard to see, and it was also starting to get very cold.

"I think there might even be a frost tonight!" said Twotone seriously.

"What, already! We are in for a bad winter then," said Muddy.

"Yes," said Shimmer. "We'd better find somewhere pretty quick. It will be too dark to look soon, and I thought I heard something moving on the other side of the waterfall."

"What is it?" asked Shade, quite alarmed,

"Probably a fox," said Muddy.

"Yes," replied Twotone, "we'd better hurry up."

And so the four fairies and the two rabbits began to search for a hole or something to hide in for the night.

"Over here!" shouted Muddy. "I've found the perfect place."

In the roots of a big pine tree was a hole that went down quite deep, and led underneath the tree itself which would keep them both dry and warm for the night,

"This is great!" said Twotone as the fairies hurried the rabbits inside, which took little persuading, and began to excavate a little to make more room.

"OK," said Muddy, "Pepper and Romany you stay here, while we go and look for some supper."

With that the four fairies headed back out of the hole beneath the roots, and began to collect dandelion leaves for the rabbits.

"Thank goodness you two always pack loads when we go on a picnic," remarked Muddy to the girls as he pulled a large dandelion leaf out by the roots.

"Yes," laughed Shimmer, "we should be fine, there's loads left."

"That will do," announced Shade, "Let's get back before it goes too dark, and the rabbits get worried." And with that, they started back to the tree.

The Fox

When they arrived back, the rabbits were indeed quite anxious, for the fox had been sniffing around, and Romany said it had even tried to dig a way in, but luckily they were well protected by the roots, and far enough under the tree for the fox not to be able to reach them.

So the four fairies made a soft bed out of some dry leaves, and gave the rabbits their supper, and feeling much calmer now that the fairies were back, the two rabbits ate up all the dandelions and then settled down into the leaves, while the fairies ate their supper.

"Do you think it will come back?" asked Shimmer.

"Probably," said Twotone quite seriously, "they don't give up that easily."

"Well if it does, we'll be ready for it," said Muddy with a determined tone.

"What shall we do?" asked Shade anxiously.

"Don't worry," said Twotone, "it can't get at us anyway, the only thing we have to worry about is the rabbits panicking and running away from the safety of the tree."

And so feeling quite safe in their cosy little hideaway, the four fairies chatted and shared out the picnic, saving some for breakfast the next day.

By now it had gone very cold outside, and there was indeed a ground frost. The fairies had just decided to settle down for the night when suddenly they heard a scratching sound coming from above!

"Quiet!" whispered Muddy.

"What is it?" asked Shade and Shimmer, very alarmed.

"I thought I heard something outside."

"The fox, I bet," said Twotone, "we'd better go and see."

"Yes," said Muddy, "stay with the rabbits, while Twotone and I have a look."

"Be careful," exclaimed Shade, "foxes are very crafty, especially when they are hungry and can smell rabbits."

"Don't worry," replied Muddy, "It won't catch us."

With that the two fairies crept up to the entrance of the hole and peered out into the frosty night. It was very cold and a thick mist had formed over everything, making it hard to see, and a full moon shone down onto the mist, giving everything a creepy eerie feeling

"Over there," whispered Twotone.

"Yes, I can see him," replied Muddy quietly.

The fox was around the side of the tree, sniffing through the undergrowth.

"I'll sneak outside and try to attract his attention," said Muddy, still whispering,

"How are you going to do that?" asked Twotone, quite alarmed at the prospect.

"I don't know yet," replied Muddy, "but I'll think of something."

And with that he flew very quickly out of the

hole. Meanwhile the fox had heard the commotion and was on his way around the tree to see what was going on.

"Well that was easy," thought Muddy as he saw the fox appear at the entrance of the hole, but what he wasn't expecting was the fox to totally ignore him, and proceed to stick his nose down the hole where Twotone was hiding, and start to dig to his heart's content.

"Hey, over here, you bushy tailed barm pot!" shouted Muddy very sternly. The fox looked up, alarmed, as it hadn't even seen Muddy, who was waving a big piece of dry bracken at him. The fox, now angry and hungry, lunged forward towards Muddy, who shouted bravely, "Come on, and catch me if you can!"

And with that he promptly dropped the bracken

and shot off at high speed, dodging the trees as he went, closely followed by the fox, and all poor Twotone could do was watch helplessly at the entrance of the hole as Muddy quickly disappeared from view.

Muddy's Flight of Fear

"What's going on?" came a voice from behind Twotone. The girls had come to see where they had got to.

"Muddy's only gone and lured the fox away on his own," said Twotone, sounding horrified. "Hope he will be OK, you can't see a thing out there, and there's bound to be more than one fox in this forest, not to mention badgers or even worse, owls. The fool, he should have waited for me. Two pairs of eyes are better than one, there's nothing I can do now but wait and hope he finds his way back in one piece. You go back down to the rabbits, girls, there's no point us all freezing to death out here. I'll let you know as soon as he comes back."

"If he comes back!" said Shade, nearly on the point of tears.

"Of course he will come back, don't let's talk like that!" said Shimmer very crossly. "Come on Shade, let's go and get warm. Muddy's not stupid, he's just silly that's all."

Meanwhile, when Muddy thought he had lured the fox far enough away, he flew high into the air, and the fox was left jumping up and down at the bottom of a very big tree.

"That should do it," laughed Muddy as he began to make his way back. "Now then," he thought to himself, "hich way was it?"

As he stood looking around him, trying to get his bearings, he remembered passing a large odd shaped holly bush, which he could see faintly in the distance as the moonlight cast its shadows off the curly leaves.

"There you are," he thought as he made his way towards it, "now I know where I am." But what he hadn't seen were two beady eyes studying his every move. As Muddy made his way quickly towards the holly bush his senses told him that something was wrong, something was watching him, but the mist was so thick that Muddy struggled to see anything, and yet he knew he was in danger, that something was out there. So with all his senses working overtime he crept closer to the holly bush.

"Nearly there," he thought, as the holly bush

cleared the mist, but just then he heard a loud rushing sound, and turned around sharply to see the talons of a large tawny owl coming at him very fast. Luckily Muddy's reactions were even faster.

"Conscious Shatter" he shouted, and the owl momentarily dropped from the sky as the stunning spell took effect. Muddy managed to dodge it by a whisker, as, shaking with fear, he shot into the holly bush for cover!

"Oh boy that was too close for comfort," said Muddy to himself, still shaking, "think I'd better get back and quickly."

After waiting for quite a while to make sure the coast was clear, Muddy nervously made his way back through the dark and gloomy forest, all his senses still working overtime.

"Are you all right?" shouted Twotone as Muddy

came in sight.

"Yes, perfectly," replied Muddy, relieved to see Twotone come charging out from the hole in the roots. "I don't think he will be back, but just in case I think we should cast ourselves a protection enchantment to ward him, or any other unwelcome visitor off."

"Good idea," said Twotone. "I'll get the girls; we are going to need Shade's expertise for that."

And so the four fairies formed a circle at the entrance of the hole and said altogether, "Purely with good intention we cast this circle of protection!"

Then while Muddy and Twotone kept watch, Shade and Shimmer went back down under the tree to keep the rabbits company, and as dawn was about to break, Twotone and Muddy finally joined them, and fell fast asleep snuggled up to the rabbits.

The next day was bright and crisp, and Shade and Shimmer were the first ones out and about. They made up two hammocks, which would be harnessed to the rabbits, and used to carry the two heavy bundles of sticks back to Bramblefrost village. They collected more dandelions for the rabbits, and after breakfast they loaded up and started for home.

"Well, never a dull moment, eh!" joked Muddy, as they strolled along.

"No," said Twotone, with a wry smile on his face. "When I saw you waving that bracken at the fox, I thought you'd lost your senses!"

"Well," said Muddy seriously "All I could see was that fox with his head stuck down the hole where you were hiding! So I had to do something, didn't I?"

"Yes," said Twotone, "very brave I must say, just wait until we tell the others!"

And as the four fairies and two rabbits neared home, they were welcomed by the whole village. They had not been the only ones caught out by the twilight, so there were going to be some interesting stories told that night at the gathering, However, it had been worth it, as all the fairies, with a little help from their friends, had collected record amounts of dry wood, which they turned into a big store of charcoal, enough to keep them warm even in the very bitterest of winters.

GHOSTLY GOINGS ON

Yet deeper into autumn we go.

There was a faint, damp mist hanging over everything, so it was no wonder that there was a spooky feeling about Bramblefrost Manor. When the fairies heard tell of a strange white object that had been seen up at the Manor, word soon spread that it was, in fact, a ghost! Although Granit was not convinced, all the other fairies decided not to go up past the Manor on their own.

So to that end, Twotone, Muddy, Shade and Shimmer teamed up as usual to go and collect a tooth from a little boy in a nearby village. The only thing was, the village was on the other side of Bramblefrost Manor, and so the fairies would have to go right past it in order to get there.

Now fairies are not easily frightened, but this ghost thing had got them all a bit jittery. Twotone and Muddy bravely said that they would lead the way, so with their lanterns brightly shining they headed off up the winding gravel drive towards theManor.

As they got near, their eyes were peeled for signs of anything unusual, but the mist was so thick around the Manor they couldn't see much at all, and so they slipped silently past hand in hand.

"Nothing," said Muddy with a faint sound of disappointment in his voice.

"Thank goodness," replied Shade and Shimmer.

"It's probably just that stupid mole seeing things! After all his eyesight isn't brilliant!" said Twotone, sounding rather annoyed at having shown himself to be a little afraid in front of the girls.

And so thinking the mole was obviously wrong, they collected the tooth, which was a good one, and so worth all the effort, then started back towards the Manor, this time chatting away to each other, oblivious to the creepy surroundings.

Just then Shimmer stopped.

"Can you see that?"

"Don't you start," said Twotone, sounding alarmed, and looking in the direction Shimmer was pointing her lantern.

"Yes," said Muddy "I can see something!"

"What is it?" asked Shade with an obvious quiver in her voice,

"I don't know, but I am going to find out!" replied Muddy, and with that he began to creep through the tall grass at the edge of the big lawn.

Through the mist they could faintly see something white and it seemed to be moving.

"The mole was right after all," whispered Twotone, who sounded very alarmed.

"I am not so sure," said Muddy, "We have to get closer."

"Not on your Nelly," replied Twotone, "I vote we should all scarper while we still can!"

"No," said Shimmer, "otherwise everyone will think that we are afraid."

"But we are, aren't we?" replied Shade, her voice still quivering.

"No we are not!" said Muddy proudly. "Come on, follow me."

And so the four fairies crept ever closer to the strange white thing floating up and down by the big cedar tree, but as they got closer and the mist cleared a little bit, they could see what it was that they were all afraid of.

"It looks like a bird," said Twotone, very relieved.

"Yes," said Shimmer, "It's a dove."

The fairies all felt quite silly now.

"Well that explains it," said Muddy, "but why is a dove out at this time of night? We'd better go and see what the matter is."

And so the four fairies approached the distressed dove to see if they could help.

"Are you all right?" asked Shimmer, quite concerned,

"Oh no not really," said the dove, who then introduced himself. "My name is Spirit, [which was quite apt given the circumstances] and I have been locked out of my Aviary for nearly a week.

You see, I panicked when the man from the Manor came to clean us out, and I flew past him, but since then I have returned every night to see if by chance the door would open, but no, it's hopeless. I shall never get back in."

The four fairies looked at each other in amazement.

"You are so lucky to have been able to survive a week on your own, you know!" exclaimed Muddy.

"Don't worry," said Twotone hastily. "We will help you, won't we?"

"Of course," said the others.

So the four fairies lost no time and went straight to the wood shed where they had seen old George the gardener put all his things before returning to the manor. While Shade and Shimmer kept an eye out, Muddy and Twotone found a way in through a broken window. Once inside the two fairies searched for where the keys to the Aviary were kept, and sure enough inside a cupboard marked "PRIVATE KEEP OUT" were all sorts of different bunches of keys, each tied up with string and fixed with a tag stating what they were for.

"Here they are," announced Muddy. "Look, it says 'Aviary',"

"Good," said Twotone, "Let's go."

Struggling to carry the heavy bunch of keys, the four fairies headed back through the misty night to help Spirit get back into his home. Spirit was waiting for them in anticipation.

"Thank you so much," he said gratefully, as the fairies struggled to open the door.

"If there is ever anything I can do for you, don't

hesitate to ask."

"That's OK," said Shimmer "We were glad to help."

Feeling quite proud of themselves they watched as Spirit was greeted back into the Aviary by all his friends.

"Well that's us done for the night, I believe!" said Twotone, quite relieved.

"Yes," replied Muddy "I think we have solved the mystery of the ghostly goings on— let's go home and tell everyone over a nice cup of honey tea."

CHAPTER FOUR

WINTER AT BRAMBLEFROST

The New Hall

It was early December and the ground had been frozen hard for weeks, Granit had warned that this winter was going to be a cold one, so the Bramblefrost fairies were well prepared for it. They were lucky to live where they did, as Bramblefrost Manor had a well-stocked garden full of herbs, winter vegetables and lots more yummy things that the fairies from other villages would have had to travel miles to find. It was no wonder that Bramblefrost village had lots of visitors around this time of year.

The whole village had been working hard on a new hall beneath a large oak tree just inside the grounds of Bramblefrost Manor. It was going to be a grand affair. The rabbits from a nearby field had helped to dig out a really big chamber, and the fairies had then built the walls from teeth they had been collecting all year. which they then lined with oak panels on both the walls and the floor. They put in two fireplaces, one at each end of the room, just to make sure they would be warm and cosy, and finally the walls were decorated with bright lanterns.

"This is going to be great," remarked Muddy as he stood looking around at his handiwork. He had a talent for woodwork that was the envy of many.

"Yep, it sure is," replied Twotone, "I wonder if we will get a visit from the Meadowsweet lot this year?"

"Oh, bound to" said Muddy, "especially when they hear of our new hall, and the record amount of food Granit has stored away!"

Just then Shade and Shimmer came down the steps with a tray of freshly baked fairy cakes and a pot of dandelion tea for the workers.

"Wow!" exclaimed Shimmer, "we are going to have the best Christmas Eve party of all time, this is fantastic!"

"Oh yes," agreed Shade, "the hall looks wonderful, so cosy with both of the fires lit."

"Indeed," replied Muddy, "so just think what it will look like when we decorate it with a big tree, holly and ivy and lots more candles— you'd better get busy making those candles, Twotone, we don't want to run out."

"Oh don't you worry, Muddy, I've got a good store of them, all different colours too!"

The hall was going to be officially opened by Granit on Christmas Eve, and all who came would be made welcome, and invited to join in with the traditional Christmas party. This year was going to be the best yet, as everyone had been busy making all sorts of cakes, jams, pickles, and a special Christmas treat that had been brewing for a whole year. You see, the fairies had been given a record amount of honey that spring, and it had been kept topped up all year, thanks to the helpfulness of Muddy, Twotone, Shade and Shimmer. So Faz, who was particularly good at making fruit wine, was given the task of turning all that honey into mead, and all the fairies were looking forward to sampling it on Christmas Eve!

One particular morning just before Christmas Eve, it was so cold that only a brave few ventured out at all, but that didn't stop Muddy and Twotone persuading the girls to go and try a spot of ice skating on the now frozen solid bird bath in the grounds of Bramblefrost Manor.

"We will bring the soup and sandwiches and you two can bring the tea and cake," Muddy said as he got out his woolliest jumper, "then we won't get too cold will we?"

"You speak for yourself," muttered Shimmer, still not sure whether it was a good idea, and trying to remember where on earth she had put her lambswool gloves.

And so all wrapped up in their warmest clothes and with hot soup, warm bread and cakes packed into their knapsacks, the four fairies headed for the big birdbath.

The landscape was white with frost and as they chatted away to each other their breath made white clouds in the air, and even their tiny little feet made delicate crunching sounds as they walked along.

"Do you think it will snow?" asked Shimmer.

"Granit seems to think so, he had me making more sledges just in case, and Flint has been making more harnesses for the rabbits," replied Muddy.

"Well there's nothing like travelling in a one rabbit open sleigh, is there?" laughed Shade.

"Except when you are racing with them!" Shimmer replied excitedly.

You see, if it snows, Bramblefrost village meets up with other nearby villages in the valley beyond the woods, and has rabbit racing competitions—these are highly skilled, and the winners are treated like celebrities! Both Shade and Shimmer had won their races with ease the previous year and had become very popular, especially with two of their rivals from the Meadowsweet village, called Moss and Thorn, much to the annoyance of Muddy and Twotone!

"Well, let's hope it does snow then," said Muddy, looking at Twotone with a wry smile.

"We would like another chance to show off our sleigh racing skills, eh Twotone?"

Twotone just smiled and said, "Look, we're here, let's have some warm soup before we start, it's freezing!"

And so the four fairies enjoyed a nice mug of hot soup with warm bread, before putting on their skates and flying up onto the frozen bird bath.

"My goodness," said Shimmer. "It's frozen solid, there's no chance of the birds getting a drink from here!"

"No, that's true," replied Twotone, "Muddy and I will put some fresh water out when we give them the left over bread later."

"Yes," replied Shimmer, "I think it would be a good idea to do that every day while the weather is this cold."

The fairies all nodded in agreement, then started skating around the table, going faster and faster, dodging each other as they went, and laughing so much they could hardly see. Muddy, showing off his backward moves at high speed, promptly fell off the back of the bird table, and just managed to stop himself hitting the deck by a whisker. A little embarrassed, he sprung back onto the table and said, "Of course, I've been practising that move for ages!"

"Of course," said the others in unison, trying not to laugh.

After a while the fairies were out of breath with dodging and laughing until Shade shouted "Enough!" Still laughing, she sat down on the edge of the bird table closely followed by the others.

"That was great fun, Jack Frost would be hard pressed to beat that skating," Shimmer said as she passed out the rest of the picnic.

"See, I told you you'd enjoy yourself," replied Muddy, tucking into a large slice of fairy cake. "Twotone and I always come up with the best ideas, isn't that right Twotone?"

Twotone just smiled and drank his dandelion

tea.

Shade exclaimed, "Look it's starting to snow!" And sure enough, big juicy flakes of snow began to fall.

"Looks like you will get the chance to test your skills in the sledge after all Muddy," said Twotone, still smiling.

"Yep, very true, and talking of sledges, at least this means the big fella won't have any trouble getting here tomorrow night; if this keeps up he won't need our help at all," replied Muddy excitedly. "Let's get back to the village before it gets too bad."

By the time the four reached home, the ground was covered in snow and quite a few of the village were over on the other side of the hedge, having snowball fights. Everyone was excited.

In the afternoon Muddy, Twotone, Flint, Faz, Bracken and Birch all went into the woods to get a branch from a big pine to use as their Christmas tree, and also to collect holly and ivy to decorate the hall. When they had finished putting everything up, Twotone fetched the stack of candles he had made for the occasion, and so the finishing touches were completed as the light began to fade.

As the boys walked back home, the hedge in which Bramblefrost village stood was now covered in a thick layer of snow, which made all the lanterns on each little house shine with a cosy glow.

"Seems a shame to go in tonight," remarked Twotone, as they neared their front door, "it's quite magical."

"Yeah," said Muddy, "it is," and they stood in silence for a moment and watched the twinkling lanterns dotted all through the hedge. "Just like a string of fairy lights, eh?"

"Oh very funny," smiled Twotone as he opened the door.

The big race

It was the morning of Christmas Eve and the snow had steadily fallen all night. The fairies awoke to a bright crisp day, and as Twotone and Muddy made their way along the cheerfully lit village to Shade and Shimmer's cosy little house, everyone seemed to be out and about. Most were ferrying goodies to the hall in readiness for the big party that night, and when the boys arrived they were just in time for tea and toast.

"Timed that right, didn't you?" Shade said as she opened the door. "Come in, we won't be long."

Taking off their coats, Muddy and Twotone followed Shade into the kitchen where Shimmer sat toasting fresh bread on the fire.

"Is it cold out?" inquired Shimmer as the boys sat down at the table.

"Freezing," replied Muddy excitedly, "I wonder what time we will have the races?"

"We'll find out when we get to the hall I suppose," said Shade, "Granit will have been in touch with the other villages by now, no doubt."

"How exciting to have the races today on Christmas Eve of all days," Shimmer said, passing the toast and butter to the boys, "What with the race, the new hall and party in one day, this year is going to be hard to follow!"

After the four had eaten several slices of toast and drank a whole pot of tea, they gathered up the cakes, biscuits and sandwiches that they had made for the party and headed off for the hall, where the whole village was gathering, everyone waiting to see if Granit had heard from the other villages. As Shade and Shimmer put their goodies on the long, overflowing table which ran the whole length of the back wall, Shade said, "I can only just fit our offerings on here, how many are we expecting at this party?"

"Yes it's a bit full, isn't it?" replied Shimmer.

Just then Granit came down the steps into the hall. "Can I have your attention everyone," he said as he made his way to the right hand fire place at the far end of the hall. He paused for a moment and looked around, taking in how wonderful it looked now the hall was finally finished. "I must say, the hall is a sight for sore eyes, and I think we will be the envy of many villages when they see it in its full glory tonight. I am very proud of you all," he said with a bit of a lump in his throat. "Now then, the news you have all been waiting for. I am pleased to tell you that all the local villages are to meet in the valley at 11.30 this morning, so make sure you dress warmly, there will be plenty of hot soup and herb bread provided by our kind neighbours from the Meadowsweet village."

Muddy and Twotone looked at each other and tutted. "Those who wish to enter the races should go and get their rabbits and harnesses ready without delay, so good luck all, and see you there."

"Might have known the Meadowsweet lot

would be there," said Muddy grudgingly as the four headed out of the hall.

"And what's wrong with that?" asked Shade, sounding quite annoyed at the tone of Muddy's voice.

"Nothing," interrupted Twotone, casting a sideways glare at Muddy, "we are just anxious to even the score after last year's bad luck, eh Muddy?"

"Er yeah something like that," replied Muddy scornfully.

When Muddy, Twotone, Shade and Shimmer arrived in the valley it was positively buzzing. "There is definitely more here than last year," noted Shimmer as the four led their rabbits to where the Bramblefrost villagers were gathered.

"I bet word has spread about our new hall and

party," said Muddy, and they all nodded in agreement.

"Well, it makes it more exciting then," said Shade with a wry smile.

This year's course looked more challenging as well, and even Shade and Shimmer looked a bit worried. "Think we are in for a bit of fun with this course, don't you agree?" came a voice from behind them.

"Oh hello Thorn, Moss, haven't seen you for ages, how are you?" said Shimmer, smiling from ear to ear.

"We are just fine, thanks," replied Thorn, "Looking forward to testing out our skills on this course, it looks a bit challenging to say the least!"

"The very least" whispered Muddy sarcastically. Shimmer shot him a glance that would turn milk sour.

"Yes" replied Shimmer, "it should test us all right."

"Well, we'll see you on the opening round then, good luck," said Thorn as they headed for the Meadowsweet lot.

Granit and all the other elders from far and wide stood at the starting line to announce the start of the races.

"Thank you all for coming, I am sure we will all enjoy this year's races. I would like to thank all the elders for designing such a challenging course, our best yet I think, if I might be so bold. May I thank the Meadowsweet village for providing us with our refreshments today. I can heartily recommend the hot chocolate and warm gingerbread, they will definitely keep those of us just spectating warm, and will serve as a very good boost for all you competitors. May I also take this opportunity to invite you all to our Christmas Eve party, which will take place in our newly built oak hall this evening from 8 o'clock. OK, can we have our first competitors to the start please, numbers 1 to 5, thank you and good luck."

"Don't know if I'll even get through the qualifying round on this course," said Twotone doubtfully.

"Yes you will," Muddy whispered, "we can't let Thorn and Moss show us up this year. Did you see that look Shimmer gave me? We've got to show them what we're made of."

Twotone looked even more worried now.

"Oh don't worry, we'll be OK, just go steady on the qualifier. We can worry about the speed when we get through."

There were a large number of entries, due to the number of villages which were competing that year, but the course was unforgiving to even the smallest mistake, and so the numbers were significantly reduced by the end of the qualifying round.

"Well done Twotone!" exclaimed Muddy as a red faced Twotone crossed the finish line in one piece. "We are in with a chance now, half the competitors are out already."

"I don't know about that," said Twotone climbing down from his sleigh. "Thorn and Moss got through didn't they?"

"Yes they did, but Moss nearly lost it on that last bend— he came round the corner on one runner!"

"Shade and Shimmer made it look easy though, didn't they?" said Twotone with great admiration. "Yes, they already have a crowd around them, including you know who. Still we're through so let's go get ready for the next race."

"All remaining competitors must complete the next round in a time of five minutes or less," announced Granit, as the first rabbit drew up to the start. This proved to be a hard task, although Shade and Shimmer both made it without too much trouble. Thorn did the same— Moss, on the other hand, could not control his rabbit and he missed the last turn altogether and ended up in a bank of snow. The crowd went wild. Then it was Muddy's turn. He showed great skill and control and finished well within the time. Finally came Twotone who also showed great skill and control and just managed to scrape through by seconds!

"Third and final round," announced Granit. "This round will be timed and whoever has the fastest round will take home this beautiful crystal rabbit and six bottles of the finest mead, made by the talented wine maker Faz of our own Bramblefrost village. But don't despair for those of you who do not win, there will be plenty of our mead for sampling at the party tonight. Thank you, now will the seven remaining competitors make their way to the starting point please, your names will be called when it is your turn. Good luck."

The course was now lined with spectators from beginning to end, leaving the refreshment tents abandoned completely. Twotone looked quite pale as his name was the first one called out.

"Good luck", said Muddy, "and don't panic!"

"Don't panic," thought Twotone as he gave his rabbit one last pat before climbing on his sleigh. "He must have nerves of steel." He made his way through the cheering and shouts of good luck until he reached the start, then the bell rang, and off he went, faster than he had ever gone before. They positively flew over the course and as they crossed the finish line he couldn't believe they'd got through in one piece. He was shaking when he finely managed to stop, and was mugged by the crowd as he got off his sleigh. Everyone from Bramblefrost village came running over and Bracken said, "That was an amazing run Twotone, you did it in three minutes fifteen seconds!"

"Did I?" asked Twotone, astonished. "Well, at least I didn't show myself up," he thought to himself.

Next to go was Amber from the Waterfall village— she also had an impressive run and came in at a time of three minutes forty-five seconds. Then it was Thorn from Meadowsweet. Twotone watched his run with interest, not daring to breathe at some points.

"That was fast," said Bracken, sounding disappointed.

"Three minutes twenty seconds," came the announcement.

"Nice," said Bracken with a big smile.

Shade was next to go and she had a really good run but came in at three minutes twenty-five seconds. As she came over to where everyone stood, she looked a little disappointed, but nevertheless said, "Well done Twotone, what a run that was, going to be hard to beat."

"Thanks," said Twotone "but it's a long way from over yet."

Barley from the Hillswood village was next up, but the lad lost it on the last bend, and was bitterly disappointed with a time of four minutes flat. Shimmer came next and she effortlessly shot around the course, almost making it look easy. Twotone and Shade held their breath, when, three minutes and seventeen seconds later, came the announcement.

"What!" exclaimed Twotone, "I would have sworn she was faster!"

As Shimmer came over, she was smiling. "Just Muddy then, eh Twotone? You've done extremely well."

Twotone blushed slightly. High praise indeed,

he thought, coming from Shimmer, who was by far the better sleigh driver in his opinion.

Muddy started down the course like a complete lunatic, snow spraying all the spectators as he flew past. All the Bramblefrost villagers held their breath, then on the last treacherous bend he lost control and almost tipped his sleigh over, but he still came in at a respectable three minutes fifty two seconds.

"Brave," remarked Shimmer, "but stupid."

The crowd went mad, all vying for Twotone's attention, until Granit called for silence.

"I am very proud to announce that this year's winner of the rabbit race is none other than Twotone from our own Bramblefrost village."

Twotone, who was not used to such notoriety, modestly accepted the crystal rabbit from Granit and the other elders, and said, "Thank you very much, it was more luck than judgement really, but my rabbit was a good boy and ran his heart out, he will be getting a big basket of veggies from me, as well as the ones he's won."

Twotone positively glowed as he showed off the crystal rabbit to the rest of Bramblefrost village, who were all cheering and patting him on the back.

"May I remind you all that you are welcome at our Christmas Eve party tonight, and now it seems we have a double celebration?" said Granit proudly, "We hope to see you all there later, thank you."

The Christmas party

By the time everyone had got back to the village and seen that all the rabbits were well taken care of, it was 3.-30 in the afternoon, and the light had already begun to fade.

Lanterns were lit early, and there was magic in the air once more. Muddy was contemplating what to wear for such a special occasion.

"Got to look my best tonight," he remarked, "Don't want to show my best mate and winner of the most difficult race on record up, do I?"

"Give over!" said Twotone, a little embarrassed. "You mean you don't want Moss and Thorn looking anywhere near as good as you, don't you?"

"Erm, well us anyway, not that they will, because all eyes will be on you tonight, that should put a flea in their ear," said Muddy with a wry smile.

The girls were also trying on dresses and shoes, one after the other, trying to decide what to wear. "Decision made," announced Shimmer, "I am going with the baby pink and cream."

"Yes," said Shade, "It complements your blonde hair a treat. I think I will go with Christmas red."

"Good choice," said Shimmer, "Red with black hair, nothing goes better."

The hall was buzzing with activity once more. The fires were stoked and all the candles, both those on the tree and in the lamps, were lit and the room was full of colour. The band practised by playing carols, and a garland of ivy was placed across the main entrance, ready for the big opening.

As Twotone and Muddy came out of their front door and headed for the hall, the village was full of different faces, all dressed in their finest and chatting excitedly.

"Flipping heck Twotone, glad we put our best bib and tucker on, look at this lot, hope we can fit them all in!"

"Well the more the merrier, so they say," replied Twotone as they headed down one of the entrances. When they got inside the hall was quite full.

"I don't see Shade or Shimmer anywhere, do you?" asked Muddy, scanning the room,

"No, they're cutting it a bit fine," replied Twotone, "Granit will be doing the big opening in ten minutes, but there's Thorn and Moss over by the table."

"Well we knew they'd be here, didn't we?" said Muddy scornfully.

Just then Shade and Shimmer came in through the far entrance and both Twotone and Muddy's jaws nearly hit the floor!

"Pretty in pink, isn't she!" exclaimed Muddy.

"Who, the lady in red?" said Twotone.

The boys looked at each other for a moment, then Muddy said, "Quick, let's grab them a glass of mead before Thorn and Moss spot them!"

Hastily they headed for the big punch bowl and filled up four glasses, then began to make their way across the room to the girls.

"Hi," said the girls in unison as they saw Muddy and Twotone wade through the crowd.

"Er, you two look nice," said Muddy as he handed the girls their mead, trying not to blush, with Twotone nodding in agreement, also trying to keep his cool.

"Thanks, so do you," said Shimmer.

"Can you believe how many have turned up? It should be a good bash," said Muddy awkwardly.

"Yes, should be," replied Shimmer.

Just then Granit came down to the main entrance and the band went silent.

"May I welcome you all to the grand opening of our new hall and I hope you all have a glass of our very fine mead in your hands for the toast. Now I would like to invite our new celebrity, Twotone, to come and help me cut the garland."

There was a loud cheer, and a red faced Twotone made his way towards Granit.

"A few words perhaps, my boy," whispered Granit as Twotone approached.

"Erm, thank you all for sharing this special occasion with us, and I now declare Oak Hall officially open. Cheers!" With that Twotone and Granit cut the garland and a loud "CHEERS" filled the hall, as the band began to play.

Twotone was mugged as he tried to get back to his friends, everyone wanting to shake his hand and congratulate him on his big win. Then a red faced Amber asked if she could have the pleasure of the next dance, and grabbed Twotone's hand, leading him away, much to the annoyance of Muddy, who watched in horror as Moss and Thorn came over and asked Shade and Shimmer to do the same. Cursing, Muddy made his way to the big table and got himself another drink. "Would you like to dance?" came a quiet little voice behind him, and there stood a girl called Dusty from the

Waterfall village, who Muddy had spoken to several times but only in passing. She was dressed in a beautiful ivory feather style dress which complemented her dark chestnut hair. Muddy looked quite surprised but said, "Love to," and he led her to the dance floor where Twotone and Amber were dancing.

"Fancy seeing you here," said Muddy as they danced by. Twotone nodded and the girls gave each other a shy smile. After several more dances, Twotone asked Amber if she would like a drink and some food. When she said she would, they made their way off the dance floor to the big table, and were soon joined by Muddy and Dusty. "That was a brilliant race today, Twotone, you must be very proud— I didn't even get passed the qualifier," said Dusty.

"Thank you," replied Twotone, "I was just lucky, I think."

"Rubbish," said Muddy, "You're too modest,"

"Yes you are" agreed Amber, "That course was the most difficult yet, I think you should be very proud of yourself!"

Twotone blushed a little and suggested they find a seat.

Shimmer and Thorn were still dancing when Shade and Moss approached, looking a bit flushed. "We're going outside for a bit of fresh air, it's too hot in here," said Shade, "Are you coming?"

"Yes, can do" replied Shimmer, "but we must go and see Twotone to congratulate him at some point tonight."

"I think he's got all the congratulations he needs for now", remarked Thorn, and he nodded to where Twotone, Amber, Muddy and Dusty were sitting.

"Cosy," said Moss, smiling.

"Err, well, we don't have to go now," said Shimmer, a bit shocked, looking at Shade.

"No," replied Shade, as they headed up and out of the hall, "we'll go later, oK?"

There was a big Christmas moon lighting up the whole sky, shining down on the new snow, making everywhere glisten brightly. As the four walked along they chatted about the big race and how they'd all thought it was the most challenging ever. Moss and Thorn were very impressed with Shade and Shimmer's runs, and they were also most impressed with the hall, which they said was the best in those parts. They thought this Christmas Eve was the best they'd ever had. Just then a voice said, "Hello you lot."

Twotone and Muddy, accompanied by Amber and Dusty, came crunching through the snow towards them.

"Oh hello, we were just talking about you," said Shade.

"Nothing bad I hope?" replied Twotone.

"Oh no," said Shade cheerfully, "we just said we hadn't congratulated you yet on your big win, didn't we, Shimmer?"

"Yes," said Shimmer, "you are a star today that's for sure, Twotone."

"Well we think so too, don't we Dusty?" said Amber, giving Twotone a kiss on the cheek. Twotone blushed, and no one knew whether it was the kiss or the compliment that made him do so, because he just said, "Cold out here isn't it. Shall we go back inside?"

As the night drew to a close, Thorn and Moss walked Shimmer and Shade to their front door. Thorn invited Shimmer to visit him at Meadowsweet as soon as she could, and said goodbye for now. Moss bid goodnight to Shade and said he would love to take her out for the day to discuss enchantments, if she could find the time, so they all agreed to meet up in the not too distant future. Twotone and Muddy walked Amber and Dusty to where their villages were meeting to go home and said goodnight, and that they would keep in touch.

Christmas Day

It was Christmas morning and Shade and Shimmer

were up quite early, given the time they had gone to bed. The girls put the kettle on, then made some hot sweet porridge with cinnamon, baked apple and brown sugar, and stoked the fires, for it had been a cold and frosty night.

"Do you think Muddy and Twotone will still come for breakfast?" asked Shimmer, "we didn't see much of them last night."

"I don't see why not," replied Shade, "they always do, and I don't think they will miss our special Christmas porridge— it's tradition. I bet they are not up yet."

So the girls sat down on the rug in front of the fire with a hot mug of tea and opened their Christmas presents, and they were delighted with what they had. Twotone had made them both a set of wonderful scented candles and Muddy had carved a set of exquisite wooden bowls which were shaped like birds and butterflies to sit them in. Shimmer had made fresh scented soaps in fruit and flower shapes for all her friends and family, and Shade had made crystallised fruits and cranberry fudge. They also had blackberry wine, a lace pillowcase, a wonderful feather shawl each and some lovely lilac and lavender perfume.

"Haven't we done well?" asked Shimmer just as there was a knock on the door.

Shimmer opened the door and there stood Twotone and Muddy with two bottles of mead and some raspberry jam that Muddy had been given for Christmas.

"Merry Christmas, thought we could have some of this jam with our Christmas breakfast", said Muddy, handing the jar to Shimmer.

"And I thought you both might like a bottle of my mead as I've got enough to last all year," said Twotone with a smile.

"Thank you, Merry Christmas to you too, didn't think you would be up yet," replied Shimmer as she invited the boys in.

"What!" exclaimed Muddy, "you don't think we would miss our traditional Christmas breakfast do you?"

"No of course not!" laughed Shimmer.

So the four sat down and enjoyed a hearty breakfast, then they settled in front of the fire with a pot of honey tea and before they knew it, there were the sounds of excited voices coming from outside.

"It's dinner time already!" said Muddy, looking through the window at everyone making their way up to the hall. So with that, the four hurriedly put on their coats and ventured out into the cold, frosty morning.

"I am looking forward to this," remarked Twotone, "Faz and his family are doing the cooking this year and you know what a good cook he is."

"Oh yes," replied Shade, "I can't wait to see what we're having".

When they got to the hall the tables had been put in four rows and dressed in red and gold. Everyone was sitting down with friends and family, and there was a magical feeling in the air. All were delighted with the menu. It was hot vegetable soup with herb bread, followed by a savoury cheese tart and mushrooms with a crunchy herb and cheese topping and wedges of potato fried with onions and garlic, served with a green salad. This was followed by Christmas pudding and custard or Old English trifle, then there was a fantastic cheese board with home baked biscuits, and, of course, Faz's famous fruit wine to accompany the meal.

Granit stood up and raised his glass.

"As we celebrate this festive day, I would like to thank you all for your hard work this year— it has been a good year and a proud one, so let me just say Merry Christmas to you all!"

A loud "Merry Christmas" echoed around the hall, and the whole of Bramblefrost village tucked into their well-deserved Christmas lunch.

THE END

Lightning Source UK Ltd.
Milton Keynes UK
UKHW01f0608220618
324641UK00001B/441/P